Parents and Caregivers,

Stone Arch Readers are designed to provide enjoyable reading experiences, as well as opportunities to develop vocabulary, literacy skills, and comprehension. Here are a few ways to support your beginning reader:

- Talk with your child about the ideas addressed in the story.

- Discuss each illustration, mentioning the characters, where they are, and what they are doing.

- Read with expression, pointing to each word. You may want to read the whole story through and then revisit parts of the story to ensure that the meanings of words or phrases are understood.

- Talk about why the character did what he or she did and what your child would do in that situation.

- Help your child connect with characters and events in the story.

Remember, reading with your child should be fun, not forced. Each moment spent reading with your child is a priceless investment in his or her literacy life.

Gail Saunders-Smith, Ph.D.

Stone Arch Readers

are published by Stone Arch Books
a Capstone Imprint
1710 Roe Crest Drive
North Mankato, Minnesota 56003
www.capstonepub.com

Library of Congress Cataloging-in-Publication Data
Yasuda, Anita.
The mystery coins / by Anita Yasuda ; illustrated by Steve Harpster.
p. cm. -- (Stone Arch readers: Dino detectives)
Summary: Using Ty the Tyrannosaurus Rex's new invention, the Dino Detectives find
a bag of strange coins at the beach and trace them back to a carnival.
ISBN 978-1-4342-5972-1 (library binding) -- ISBN 978-1-4342-6201-1 (pbk.)
1. Dinosaurs--Juvenile fiction. 2. Coins--Juvenile fiction. 3. Inventions--Juvenile fiction.
[1. Dinosaurs--Fiction. 2. Coins--Fiction. 3. Inventions--Fiction. 4. Mystery and detective stories.]
I. Harpster, Steve, ill. II. Title.
PZ7.Y2124Mys 2013

813.6--dc23   2012046961

Reading Consultants:
Gail Saunders-Smith, Ph.D
Melinda Melton Crow, M.Ed
Laura K. Holland, Media Specialist

Designer: Russell Griesmer

Printed in China by Nordica.
0314/CA21400182
022014
007226NORDF13

The Mystery Coins

by **Anita Yasuda**
illustrated by **Steve Harpster**

STONE ARCH BOOKS
a capstone imprint

Meet the
Dino Detectives!

Dot the Diplodocus

Sara the Triceratops

Cory the Corythosaurus

Ty the T. rex

Zip! Zap! Bang!

Ty is making another invention in his lab.

"It's perfect!" says Ty.

Ty calls his friends.

"Meet me at the beach," says Ty.
"I have a surprise."

"Hi, everyone!" says Ty. "This is my new invention!"

"What does it do?" asks Dot.

"It finds treasure," says Ty.

"Cool!" says Cory.

Ty turns the machine on. It starts beeping right away.

"I already found something!"
says Ty.

The dinosaurs start digging.

"It's just an old metal pail,"
says Ty. "Let's keep looking."

Soon the machine starts beeping again.

"Look what I found!" yells Ty. "A big bag of coins!"

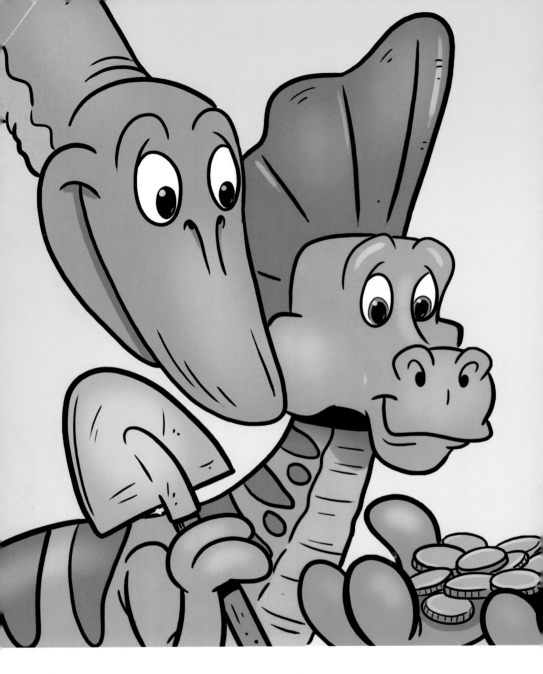

"We're rich!" says Cory.

"I've never seen coins like these," says Sara.

"It's the case of the mystery coins," says Cory.

The coins have pictures on them. One has a clown. One has a big tent. One has balloons.

"What do the pictures mean?"
asks Dot.

The dinos think and think.

"I've got it!" says Ty. "The carnival!"

"The carnival is on the other side of the beach," says Sara.

"Let's go!" says Dot.

"There are so many games!"
says Ty.

"But which one needs coins?"
asks Sara.

"It's not mini golf," says Cory.

"Or the balloon pop," says Dot.

"Look!" says Ty. "That game is closed."

"It's the coin toss game!" says Sara.

"Why are you so sad?" asks Ty.

"I lost the coins for my game," says the dino.

"Are these yours?" Ty asks. "We found them on the beach."

"Yes!" he says. "My pet hid
them in the sand. I couldn't
open my game without them!"

"Mystery solved," says Ty.
"And my invention works!"

"It sure does," says Cory. "It
found coins and a carnival."

"Come on!" says Sara.
"Let's toss some coins!"

STORY WORDS

invention   treasure   mystery

surprise   machine   carnival

Total Word Count: 286